WHAT HANDS HOLD

IF THEY HAD A VOICE

BRAD AYERS

Night Rain Books

Cover illustration: pickpic.com

Photographs by Bradford Chapman Ayers

FIRST EDITION

Printed in the United States of America

ISBN 978-1-956828-03-0

Night Rain Books / Night Rain Press
PO Box 2220
Newport, OR 97365

Night.Rain.Press@gmail.com
http://NightRainBooks.com

WHAT HANDS HOLD

CONTENTS

INTRODUCTION TO WHAT HANDS HOLD

Our hands touch and hold many things. Just today, see if you can list all the things your hands held or touched so far. Start this morning by brushing your teeth. The light switch in the bathroom had to be turned on, the toothbrush held and some toothpaste applied, the faucet knob turned to fill a glass to rinse, and a towel taken from the rack to dry the hands. That is 6 just in the first few minutes after waking up, not to mention the assorted other subtle touches along the way to the bathroom.

But in these stories, we are looking for something more. We will be looking at some of the special things your hands do. Not just the routine daily chores. Those few things that your hands have held with special meaning sometime in your lifetime. Ones that most of us can relate to no matter who in our modern society we may be. So, as you read, stop when you remember one especially important to you. What story does it tell?

We will limit these stories to the good things our hands do with the things they touch and hold. Nothing too embarrassing, or sinister, or specialized, but things with emotion and passion for the holder. A full range of hand experiences from the early days and on along the human lifetime. And keeping with the Voices Books's focus, the stories will be told by objects the hands are holding and touching.

These stories will get you thinking about what was, could have been, and maybe even where your hands should be going next. Places, people, things, events, expressions, symbols, jobs, games, and so many it makes the mind work hard to catch up with what the hands are doing. Quite a job our hands do for us. Let's see if you can find something to remember.

1

THE RING FINGER

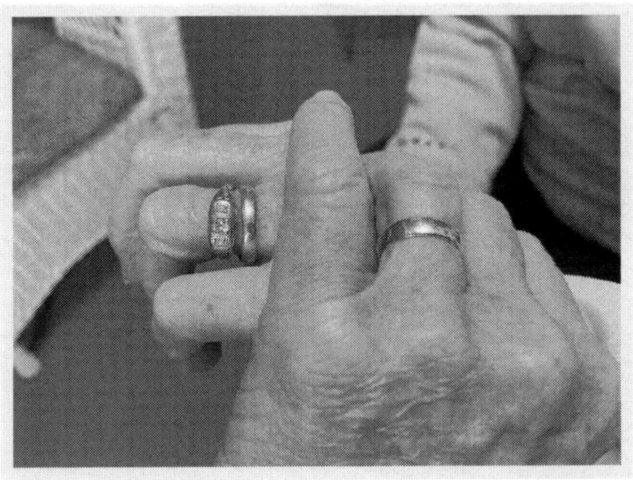

SHE STANDS IN A BEAUTIFUL WHITE WEDDING DRESS READY TO WALK slowly down the church isle.

The wedding rings are held securely by bridesmaid and best man standing ready at the altar.

Yes, we are talking about a wedding ring, and I am the groom's ring speaking.

This is my story.

I was bought by the bride to be placed on the groom's left hand ring finger during the wedding ceremony. I am a simple, yet elegant, polished and smooth, slightly curved on top, gold band. I have a single phrase engraved inside. The wedding date to memorialize the wedding, and the pledge of her lifelong love.

One hand to the other will soon complete the bond. The rings to be worn on hands for a lifetime. But first, the hands of the bridesmaid and best man have a very important job. Hold the rings securely and be ready to hand the rings to the bride and groom. The groom, trying to settle his nerves, stands waiting at the altar as the bride approaches. His hands are a little tense which creates a slight swelling.

My life as a ring started with raw materials and a skilled craftsman. I have been through many hands during my creation, so I am used to being held, but never worn as intended this day. I am held securely now. The bridesmaid's and best man's hands are relatively calm and gentle, yet secure as to not let their precious treasures slip.

I suspect things will get a little more tense when the moment arrives.

The wedding music begins. An 1842 Mendelssohn music composition, now known as the "Wedding March", is being played. Centuries of history and tradition between then and now have been called upon once again. The music cascades and surrounds us from somewhere unseen. I see the groom glance at the best man who opens his hand slightly to reveal the bride's ring to the groom as assurance it is secure. The bride gets the same assurance from her bridesmaid where I rest.

The wedding ceremony goes mostly as planned. I listen intently awaiting my turn. The minister, with close up communications, reassures in a soft whisper to the wedding couple, everything is going to be fine. They try to relax, but their nerves have their way today.

And then the moment arrives. The minister is asking the bride for my ring. I am handed carefully to the bride. She holds me so tenderly. Touching me as if I were the most precious thing she has ever held. I don't think I will ever have such a tender, warm, and sure hand around me ever again. I almost don't want to leave. Yet my purpose is not yet fulfilled.

"Place the ring," the minister is saying.

The rest of the words fade into the emotions of the minute. The groom places the bride's ring first. All going well so far. The groom holds out his left hand to receive me. I can see he is a little unsure exactly where his hand should be, but the bride reaches to steady. Then, holding me between several fingers she finds his ring finger, and I start my final journey. We begin smoothly down the ring finger but at the second finger joint I notice we are stopping. I get a stronger push, but I am still not going any further. The swelling of excitement has me stuck. The bride tries again, but I am just not going on.

What does this mean? Is my full intended purpose not going to be realized?

And just then the groom reaches with his right hand to finish pushing me onto his ring finger, exactly where I was intended to rest. The bride lets out a very quiet sigh and her blush begins to soften.

Perhaps that is how it will be in life. Nothing will be totally one-sided. It will always take two to make the most important things work.

And now, 62 years later, I am still on the same ring finger I was placed on that day.

I am proud of the job I have done.

2

TITLEIST RED 4

I am a golfer's dream. One swing—and in the hole.

You guessed it—A HOLE IN ONE!

I am a Titleist golf ball. An older model not sold anymore, but state-of-the-art back in 2000 when I went in on one shot that October day in Arizona. I have been retired now for some 24 years. I am proudly kept in a golf memory box with assorted tees, score cards from long ago rounds, including the one with me in it, and ball markers of various shapes, a few colorful logo golf balls, and other golfing memorabilia. I get taken out every few years for a few minutes, held in your hand again as you look for the words written on me. You read them silently and replace me.

I live a very comfortable retirement life. You will see why shortly.

Of all the things you could hold in your hands, perhaps none quite comes up to the emotions of a pre-shot golf routine about to start. I am unconsciously turned over in the hand several times as we wait. I am usually checked for grass stains or other markings that somehow my golfer superstitiously thinks might adversely affect my performance. My golfer always marks his ball a certain way. On this particular day, I was carefully marked with a simple black dot under my red number 4.

We are standing on the number 6 tee box waiting for the green to clear of the foursome ahead. We are about to tee off on a 161-yard par 3. Over the first 5 holes we were one over par. Not bad for a 7 handicapper. In fact, a fairly good start when you think about it. So perhaps a little extra handling of me reflected the building expectation of a good round brewing.

Before I take flight, let me pause a few moments to explain why a golf ball is something a hand pays particular attention to. First, I am perfectly round and covered with dimples. I may seem flawless, but the most technical golfers will test a ball's roundness by using various balancing and center of gravity techniques to see if one side repeatedly turns up. If so, the ball is rejected as being off center and might cause a putted ball to roll out of line on the green. In golf, that missed putt may make a big difference. And some golfers will even reject a ball if marked or nicked slightly. And, call it discrimination, but some golfers won't even play a found ball or ones not exactly like their current favorite brand and model. I am sure there are many more superstitions, but you get the point. A golf ball is special and not to be taken for granted.

OK—here we go. Green is clear. I am placed on a tee just above the grass line. Just high enough to ensure the selected club for the shot, a 6 iron, will clear on its downward swing. I'm lined up carefully, with the correct positioning of the word Titleist in a straight line to the flag stick. Why is this alignment important? The golfer suspects it might somehow cause a miss hit, or more likely it is just another one of those superstitions we golf balls must endure. They say anything slightly amiss to the golfer's confidence will cause trouble. And then just when I have settled into the tee to rest, I am compressed with the clubhead hit and sent skyward. As I take off, I can tell it was a good hit. I am spinning backwards, straight and true, at a fast rate, gaining altitude and distance. Golfers call this trajectory. Up, and up, and then dropping downward approaching the green. Softly landing and spinning to … OK, I know the rest, and so do you. I come to rest at the bottom of that 4 and ¼ inch diameter hole with the flag stick in it, 161 yards from my starting point. Yes, I was going the right direction and speed to drop in, even with the pole in the hole. Any faster, or even slightly offline, and I would have rimmed the cup or hit the pin and bounced away.

My golfer approaches the green looking for me and yells to one of the other golfers that I must have gone over the green. They saw me land on the green but then disappear. Visually, from 161 yards, it looked like I had rolled off the back side. So, without checking the hole first my golfer goes to the back of the green.

But no ball is found. He says to his playing partners, "could it be...?" and returns to check the hole.

There I am, just as proud as can be. A hole-in-one from 161 yards!

The foursome celebrates with "high fives."

As my golfer lifts me from the hole, I know I am going to be held in those hands more carefully and with more emotion than ever before. It is a very rare occurrence in the golfing world. Not many golfers have been so fortunate. But my golfer and his trusted Titleist Red 4 (me) are always going to be special. After the round I am marked with the event and placed in retirement. With this stimulating momentum, my golfer went on to card an even par 72 that lovely October 2000 day.

Have your hands ever felt a more perfectly round and balanced golf ball?

I am still here in the memory box to be held again and again when needed.

3

YOUR CAR KEYS

A PIECE OF METAL, CUT JAGGED ALONG ONE SIDE.

About 2½ inches long with a hole in one end.

I could go on and on about the metal used and other particulars, but I am just an old-fashioned car key. Not sounding too arrogant, I am the most important key you have most days. And don't let my simple appearance deceive you. Even though I'm like a lot of other keys you have, I am the only one that can start your car. You use me almost every day—several times, and sometimes many times. Without me you don't go anywhere very easily. I can make you late when you misplace me or forget where you put me. Some try to guard against this by having a designated hook, bowl, or countertop to put me. Others just drop me down on the first flat surface along their path, or someplace where they are sure to remember where I am.

"Now, where are my keys?"

Let's look at the hands in all this key business. I can usually only be used correctly if your hands cooperate. I may be the one thing you have in your hands most often every day. And then as I think about it, I may actually be in a tie or close second with your pen, your mouse, your cell phone, or something else you could be using. Not that all these other things aren't important, but they can't start your car, can they!

So why are we talking about car keys anyway? We don't seem to have made any great statements about car keys. And perhaps that is what is most important about us. We car keys are mostly taken for granted. We are just tossed around and handled roughly many times. We are often lost for precious minutes in the bottom of purses, pockets, jackets, and so many places it would take all day trying to list them. We have been used or misused in a hundred or so places and situations. Take for instance opening something like an envelope or plastic package or a can or bottle. We have been used to pry something open, itching and scratching, and even used as a poor substitute for a saw. Some have even been broken off trying to force open a frozen car door lock. In all of our uses we have even done our share of getting you out of a tough spot. So, go ahead and take us for granted, but we know some shady little secrets about you.

Even though we usually go through our life being taken for granted, there was one time when I was so very important. I was the key to the kingdom, so to speak. You know where and what I am talking about. Yes—the first time we met. I was the key to your brand-new car. I was held so tenderly in your hand that day. You pushed me gently into the starter lock and turned. You were not sure how hard, or when turned enough. But then it happened—your brand-new car started. I was a key part of this special moment (pun intended). You most likely don't remember. But this day was almost as important as the day you got the front door keys for your new house. Now, for reasons only you humans can explain, the front door key and me, the car key, are likely joined on the same key ring wherever we go.

Don't get me wrong. I enjoy being your car key. For the most part we have gotten along fine. Yes, I've been tossed, lost, and misused a few times, but fortunately for both of us these were the exceptions.

"Hold me tender, hold me dear", as someone once sang. Well, not quite like that—but you get the point. Give me a little special squeeze the next time we meet.

Thanks for putting up with my complaining.

4

TEA TIME

I can hold any liquid, hot or cold.

But by far my favorite is hot tea. Second choice, hot chocolate.

I am not sure now, after all these years, how or where I came from to be your favorite teacup. I know you do, so it does not worry me. I am actually more of a mug. I don't really like those dainty little cups. They are too light, don't hold quite enough, can't keep things hot, and you can't get your hands around them when you need a warming up. I am also much easier to hold and sit down securely on most surfaces with my larger and more solid base.

I could go on and on about my superior physical attributes but why make those dainty, seldom used cups in the china cabinet feel bad. So, let's go on to the important stuff. You use me for some very essential reasons. Here are a few to get you started. I am your go-to cup for hot tea on a cold night. I make you feel warm, comfortable, and secure. I help you relax, slow down, and dream a little. You sometimes hold me with both hands, and sometimes against your chest for warmth. You smell and sip my contents carefully while I am hot. As I cool a bit, you begin to drink, but never rushed. You hold me with those hands so familiar to me. A more quiet and peaceful time is now here for you.

To be completely fair, I guess we need to include coffee, hot chocolate, and hot cider drinks. Yes, I have held all of them over our life together. I guess I am lucky you chose me. You seem to be remembering those special times quite often lately. We have had some moments over the years. Several house moves, packing and unpacking me, new cabinets and shelves to decide where I should sit, dishwashers and sinks to deal with and not get dinged, or worse. I am also so blessed to have survived being replaced by all the newcomer mugs you have brought home from vacation trips, the grocery store, and even from those annual holiday craft bazaars. Don't forget those few from Starbucks at holiday time. Yes, all so pretty and clever. They last for a few drinks, but you always return to me eventually. I am kind of like an old friend of yours that comes to call. Just when needed, I seem to be there, pushed back a bit on the shelf. But you find me.

Yes, I have always been there for you.

Over the years we have shared quite a bit. Sometimes with friends but mostly just you and me. You can, and do, tell me all your quiet thoughts. We sit together and let the past wash over us again and again. But the things I remember most are the hands that hold me. Your hands. Years ago they were so strong, and I think a little bit warmer than they are now. As the years have gone by, they seem to have lost a bit of firmness. I seem to be handled a bit more carefully these days. Seems like you are not quite as certain where I should be put or how far the counter is. But you always find my special place.

I rest when you leave, imagining your hands still around me.

Let's do it again.

Don't wait too long.

5

WHERE IS THE REMOTE?

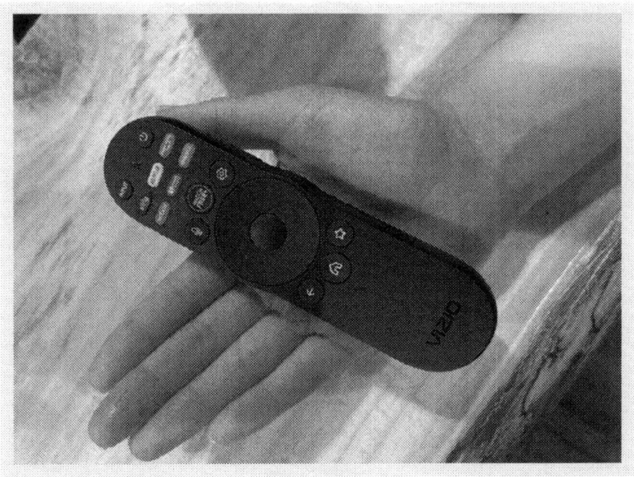

YOUR REMOTE TV CONTROL SEEMS TO HAVE A LIFE OF ITS OWN.

Yes, I do!

I am at home almost anywhere in your house. And I have been known to wander to the neighbors, take a car ride, and even go to work in your purse. But when not in your hand, I usually just lay around the house on a coffee table, chair arm, down between the sofa cushions, under some magazines or pillows, and a whole host of other locations. I like the hide and seek games we play. Almost anyplace is fair game, I guess. But I don't choose where I am put down. Your hands do.

And, you know what?

I get the blame for being lost when you can't remember where I am.

Blame your hands, not me.

Most of the time, your hands and I are really good friends. I get held quite a bit most days and in most homes. And not just by one hand but by almost as many as are living in the house. Young and old, parents and kids, gramma and gramps, even friends over for the game night. They all search for me, pass me around or demand to control me. Most hold me in the right hand, some in the left. I have seen many hands over my lifetime. Some are tender, some rather rough, and some send me tumbling across the room. Fortunately, those times are infrequent because I have been known to stop working in retaliation for the harsh treatment.

I guess I can't complain too much as I reflect on it now. I do have a warm home to live in and one of the most sought after and important jobs to do. Yes, your hands and fingers push my buttons, but I send the signals to the TV. I have the technology that makes your TV do what you want. As I see it, you are just the TV "remote jockey." You just ride along like the jockeys in the Kentucky Derby telecast we watched last week. I do all the higher-level jobs. Most of the time you don't even know how or what I am doing under your hands.

You just point and hope.

But hey, let's not argue. I was just venting a little frustration. Most of the time we are very good friends—your hands and me. I like it when you hold me, fingers moving gently over my buttons, volume controls, and direction arrows. We are a team working with all that TV technology to do exactly what we want. Well—most of the time. From my perspective you seem to be in a constant battle keeping up with it all. Channels, Cable, Dish, Wireless, Internet, Apps, Streaming, DVR, etc. And when you have a lapse, or get a new TV, or some other new service, you hold me and talk to me like we had never even met. Your hands push every button I have, confusing me, and making you so mad. READ THE INSTRUCTIONS! Some of you have even tried a "universal remote" in hopes all their problems would be solved.

But when all is said about your hands and the TV remote, we are here to stay it seems. Yes, I know, they say nothing stays the same. So, our time together may, in fact, be short in the grand scheme of things. And just as I am saying this, the groundwork for an entirely new technology is taking its first steps. Artificial Intelligence (AI) and computer chip brain implants may completely change how things are controlled. Yes, even me, your trusted TV remote control will be history.

One day you may say, "Can't the old remote come back, or even those simple knobs on the TV?"

Don't you wish for the good old days?

6

CELL PHONE CALLING

A TV IN EVERY HOME.

A computer on every desk.

A cell phone in every hand.

Now that's what our society did for us. And it took less than 75 years. Earlier in our civilization it was gas powered cars, telephones, and transistor radios. Before that steam trains, pony express, and telegraph. Further back, typewriters, electricity, and ticker tape. Further back and back, we could go. Yes, there will be a few more updates and features added trying to keep pace. But, nevertheless, just like all other past technologies, the cell phone will be obsolete somewhere during most of our lifetimes.

Go ahead and reject my argument, but this is your cell phone talking.

Do you think I would like to obsolete myself?

But enough of the history lesson. Let's have a look at today and be happy. We seem to have a love-hate kind of relationship in many cases. I'm a nice size, smooth, engineered for your hand to hold, and once mastered, very easy to use. But that may also be the first problem. The age of the hands using me seems to be a big factor in our relationship. The young hands love me but as you go up the age scale, things get progressively more confrontational, especially with older hands. Obviously the hands holding me only express what they are told to do, but hands are what I have to deal with. I get poked and tossed, lost and dropped, stolen, and broken, go for a swim, and even sky dive once in a while. All caused, in most cases, by your hands dealing with operating issues.

Get the point? I deal with a lot.

But the engineers, with their new technology obsession, and marketing, always wanting more features to compete in the market, have crammed me with a computer full of every possible convenience. Most of which you never will use. That sells new cell phones year after year, even if it makes your life more complicated. So, what choice do you have but try to keep up? Now don't get me wrong. I like being your cell phone. We have had some good times, especially with all the photos you take and share with friends. But even this seemingly simple task is sometimes a challenge for you. I get the old hand squeeze and

I hear you saying some very disgusting things about me. But I keep cool and wait for you to try again, or more importantly, get advice from the grandkids. They always make it look so easy.

Oh technology—why can't you be more friendly?

As far as hands go, I have to say you are one of the best. You hold me a lot, so we have become very good friends. I like it better than riding in your back pocket where I get the rear end of things, if you know what I mean. So, let's keep trying to be friends. I will do my best to cooperate. No, I can't guarantee satisfaction 100% of the time. You have come to discover there are electronic gremlins out there. No one knows who or what they are, but they seem to hack my functions just at a time when you are counting on me to perform. And of course, I always get the blame. Could it just be your fault, once in a while? For example, you cause static electricity just moving around—not me. And I did not walk all by myself too close to that magnet. And sometimes you accidently tap a key sequence on my keyboard causing trouble even the developer's extensive beta testing failed to catch.

Have I said it all? Only starting?

OK, let's stop fighting. Most of this is not your fault or mine.

Hold me again the way you do when things go right.

We can get through this technology house of mirrors together.

Let's just be good friends.

7

HAND-IN-HAND

Two hands, one in the other.

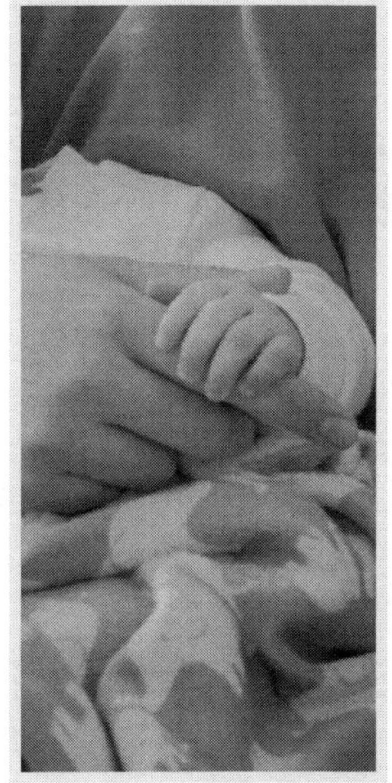

One large, one small. That's how it starts.

One of the most important stories hands tell is when one hand gets to share how it felt when held by another. And of course, the start of hand holding begins with the very newest hand.

A baby's hand. This is my hand life story.

So small I first fit inside your hand completely. I am soft and so tender you hold me with all the care you have. Just barely closing. Yet enough to feel my newborn warmth, smoothness and softness, and only a slight first movement. You don't stay too long these first few times but return often during my first few weeks. I try my best to give back when my little fingers wrap around your pinky and you feel my very first squeeze. I sense your surprise and loving reaction.

As time goes on and my hand grows to childhood size we get more friendly, with more hand holding stories yet to tell. But you will always cherish these very first times holding hands. As you look back now and search for those memories, you finally see it and live it for a moment all over again. You know how special that time was for both of us.

"Hold my hand crossing the street."

"Hold my hand, don't get lost."

These are familiar sounds as I grow up. You remember them too. Just a few examples of the many times you reached to hold my hand. Seems like I was always reaching up to find your hand too. Almost automatic at times, as we reached for each other's hands. However, there were times when I would resist, or squirm away when something tempted me. Like those times at the petting zoo and the cute little rabbits I wanted to touch, or at the grocery store with tempting things that cried out, "take me home with you."

During these early years my little hands would still fit into most any older hands. Mother, Father, Grandparents, even Aunts and Uncles, Brothers and Sisters. But on many occasions, especially during my terrible threes, I would only hold certain hands. I don't know why my hands did this. I knew all these people, but I guess it was an early show of my independence. But mostly, I willingly held my hand out when asked, and away we went.

As my hand grew through the years, I noticed less of this hand holding guidance. I guess I was growing up. But, soon enough, a new kind of hand holding was discovered. Or, perhaps I should say, another hand discovered mine? However it happened, another hand, close to my size, was reaching to hold mine. Soon our fingers were intertwining again and again. They were locked securely at times, and then on other occasions, only gently and lightly touching. As the years went on, my hands, needing warmth and caring, would reach out and again rest with another. Just as often, my hand did the warming and caring for another when needed.

Now, late in life, my little hands that once fit inside a bigger hand are now the big hands doing the holding of another small hand.

You call them your grandkids. Sometimes, great grandkids.

Perhaps handholding is our hand's most important job in life.

8

WORRY STONE

YOU MAY HAVE ANOTHER NAME FOR IT.

It may not even be a stone.

I could be a rabbit's foot, an old treasured coin, even some more modern piece of metal, stone, or wood. Almost anything really as long as it does the job. The job of easing your worries.

I am a worry stone and this is my story.

When you first picked me up, I had been lying on the beach for hundreds of years having washed there from far away. Like my other rock friends, I was once part of a larger mother rock since broke down. But that was so long-long ago. Now my mother rock is a mere shadow of herself having produced so many offspring.

You can imagine how surprised I was when you stopped and picked me up. No, you weren't the first. But that discussion might spoil your interest. So let's move on with my story. Now in your hand for the first time I was particularly interested in how you rubbed me with your thumb. Rather amazing you could hold me and rub me at the same time. You repeated this several times before putting me in your pocket.

I did not see the light of day until yesterday. I stayed in your jeans pocket after you took me to your home and changed into those sweatpants. You must have forgotten I was there. A few days later as the jeans were going into the wash you found me. You seemed a bit surprised. You held me again doing that one hand thumb rub again several times. Again and again, this time, until you put me up on your dresser top. I lay quietly for a few more days watching you occasionally pass by. But then things changed. I could sense you needed some comforting.

And that's when I went into your pocket.

And I got some paint with the word PEACE on me.

Yes, just like that picture.

We have been inseparable ever since. I go everywhere you go. Moving from one pants pocket to other pockets in the pants and shorts you wear. And I come out several times a day for your thumb rub. Sometimes at your desk, and especially at length in your stuffed family room chair. Over the years I have gotten very smooth where that thumb of yours rubs me. A slight indent has formed too. I guess you need me, and I do feel special. I must help you, but it is hard to know exactly how or why. After all, I am just a stone. I would just lay around all day if you did not move me. I don't have minerals or other active substances you might find useful. I don't play music, or sing, or even vibrate. I only get slightly warmer from your holding me. So, what is it about me you just have to have?

I guess we may never know for sure how I work for you. The only possibility is you do all the work, not me. I am like a sounding board or echo for your thoughts and feelings. You rub me, and whatever answer you need comes right back to you because you had it all the time. You just needed a friend. But there are those that strongly believe some particular stones have magic powers. I can tell you, and them, I am not magic at all.

The worry stone's power is in you. It has been there all along.

But, just in case, better keep me in your pocket.

Anyway, I like seeing new places.

9

MOUSE ALERT

DON'T WORRY.

This story is not about those furry little four-legged rodents.

I am just your friendly desk-top computer mouse.

Now, just why am I called a mouse anyway? Well, this story is not about my name, but if you need to know details, the Internet has all the answers. The short answer is I was created by an inventor trying to make computer use easier and more efficient. Before the Bluetooth we have today I had a cord to connect me. I guess some people thought I looked like a mouse with a tail.

But let's not get distracted. I am more interested in telling you what I have learned about you. Now don't get worried. I won't tell any real secrets. What I have to say is probably what any computer mouse has observed. Some of us work all night. Some work days. And some only work occasionally. But when we work we are essential to getting the results you need.

I can't do it alone.

No, I need help from you and the computer. As much as I would like to say I am the key, I am only one part of the team. I come in all kinds of shapes but generally all of us are about the same size. We fit fairly well in the palm of your hand. Some of us were designed with considerable ergonomic consideration, and others —well it is hard to tell what the designer had in mind. Regardless, we all try our best to be your (mostly) right-hand helper or sidekick, so to speak.

This story is about your hand and me. I work best if you hold me with some tenderness. I give you wrong answers if you tense up, treat me rough, move me too quickly, don't keep my batteries charged, or don't appreciate the kinds of surfaces I like to be moved around on. And I especially don't like being cursed at if my mouse arrow friend does not appear on the screen or go where you thought it should go.

I typically have two or three click functions. You have become adept at being able to use these with ease after that seemingly endless learning curve. I felt sorry for you for all those hours. But you made it, and here we are now best friends. And before I forget, let's not leave out those upstart laptops with that touch pad (some are called trackpads) trying to replace me. Notice there is no mention of a mouse. I am the only computer mouse in this story. I am the original and improved. You don't even need a hand for these others. Just a skinny finger. Gone is a place for your right hand to rest and cuddle. Is that progress?

Now, let's turn to perhaps the only real problem we have working together. I am almost hesitant to bring it up. You get so mad when this happens. But let's just get it out there and be open and honest about it.

I AM SOMETIMES RIGHT-CLICKED AT THE WRONG TIME!

There. I said it.

No, it is not my fault even though you try to blame it on me. All I did was follow your direction. I am not designed to know what you are working on. How do I know when and where to click? That's your job. My job is to perform when you tell me.

So don't try to shift the blame when you order something you did not want. Or more seriously when that email is accidently sent before proofreading has been completed, or before you check to make sure it is being sent to only the right people. But far and away, the one causing the most trouble is when you tell me to click on an unknown or bogus link that ties up your computer and then extorts you for money to fix it. That's when all #%#$@###... whatever breaks out. You almost come to the point of throwing me and the computer out the window.

Fortunately, after that one close scare, we (you) are now a little wiser.

I am again your trusted computer mouse.

Hold me in your hand.

Click me again—anytime.

10

RIGHT HAND—LEFT HAND

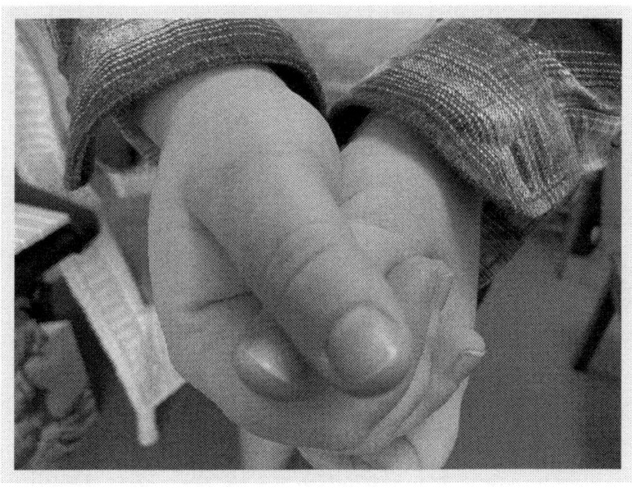

WHICH ONE GETS TO DO THE TALKING?

The right hand or the left hand?

How about one voice for both?

While you guys decide, let's get things clear. We are talking about the right and left hands of one person. Yes, each hand has our individual stories we could tell. But this story is about both of us hands holding something at the same time.

Let me clarify because I sense you may be a bit confused. Maybe you were doing something with both hands together like playing a musical instrument or eating a big slice of watermelon. It would have to be something we both hold at the same time and in the same place to make this story work.

This story is about we at the same time holding and touching each other. My official Internet research says the thing we touch the most is each other. Yes, we hold each other quite a bit and maybe more than you imagine. There are a few major reasons and a whole host of minor ones why we both do this. But yes, we two hold each other a lot.

By the way, we should clarify the hand holding in this story includes our hands together for causal touching, therapeutic rubbing, locking together for a gesture or security, finger stretching and massaging, clapping, whistling, noise making, cupping around the mouth for speaking louder or calling out, and a lot of just comfort clasping and finding a secure place for nervous hands. It includes any time both us hands touch each other with the intent of holding the other. It doesn't matter which hand starts it or ends it.

Ok, who wants to do the talking? Right or left. Oh, both of us have stories? We each do some together tasks, however many other times we have a specialty that's been developed and honed over many years that only ones does the other just watches. For example, the right hand for writing and the left hand for fingering the Ukulele keyboard. Well, you get it, but we really can't get into all the specialties each of us do so let's just concentrate on the things we do together.

Two hands on the steering wheel. Both together steering the car. Right and left, do we agree? What? Right says it is the main control and left is only for support? Left, do you agree? No? Left thinks it is just as important and can steer all itself? We get the point. Let's call it a draw. Go try playing Rock-Paper-Scissors without both of us together if you're so smart. And there you have it.

Right hand, Left hand together.

Which hand of yours is holding this book, and which is turning the page?

AFTERWORD: IF THEY HAD A VOICE

Have you ever wondered what our world has to say?

We go about our lives midst all forms of non-human objects with only a passing thought, or no thought at all about them. And rarely have we even attempted a conversation.

What if we listen closely? What would they tell us? What could we learn?

You might be surprised at just how much they have to say about us.

This series of short stories started by an impromptu response to a prompt given in a writing class I took. The prompt was to write for 14 minutes on "something you keep." Out of the blue the image of a beach rock in my hand came to mind. Probably from one of many walks on the beach at Cape Meares, and even seeing others looking for that special rock. Or even seeing someone's beach and shell collection neatly arranged or scattered around. We all have picked up a beach rock, held it a while, and maybe kept it to go home or dropped it for another.

That day I wrote about this experience, completed the assignment, and filed it away with that hint of something undone.

Several months later as I was typing my handwritten responses to past writing prompts into the computer, I again read the story I had titled, "The Hopeful Beach Rock." I lingered a while, reading it again several times. And for some mysterious reason the stories started coming one after the other about other beach objects like driftwood, waves, the ocean breeze, and more. All had something to say about us. They even ask questions and heard our thoughts. They started our memories working and recalling earlier times, ones that were happy, sad, and adventurous.

After doing several beach stories, I started to get images of other things we pass by, touch, or work with that should also get a chance to talk. Thus, started a much larger series of stories, including things we sit on, doors we go through, and a range of others you will want to read about in the Voices collections.

This is the best part. I realized that in telling these as short stories, some call flash fiction, I could give you the chance to make it your own. I give each a range of emotions and experiences, but you will find it compelling to fill in and expand with your own.

As you read the stories, remember only the non-human object does the talking. You have only to listen. The chair, for example, will ask you to remember what you were doing and thinking as you sat for a while, then suggests answers and asks even more questions. The door will recall memories of your emotions the door had observed as you passed through. Like a mirror, the door reflects these and suggests what you were thinking and whether you had any regrets. The beach rock wonders and asks you if you will keep it or discard it and choose another, leaving you to determine the outcome. Interesting life lessons for sure.

Each reader of these stories will have a unique reaction to the observations and answers to the questions because all have different experiences. The one common link is we all have these kinds of memories. And each subsequent reading will only add to the recall and variations, with even new themes and outcomes of your own.

Some stories were written on the lighter side of things, playful, and happy times. Some are more serious with only hints of deeper concerns, but none are scary or tragic. Some have a moral bent and others suggest you read between the lines to get the nuance.

Most stories, however, are just plain fun.

ABOUT THE AUTHOR

I give most of the inspiration credit to the wonderful Northwest and Oregon coast. I arrived in 2015 and have not stopped creating in new and unusual ways. It inspires all art forms, and frankly just about anything you want to do. So, I give thanks for a second chance to prosper including my efforts of fiction writing and just recently song writing.

After a first degree in Fine Arts from California State University, I went into business for my professional life. An MBA from the University of Denver followed while working for three major US companies, then running and starting my own along the way.

Concurrent to the business side, I was an adjunct professor in the MBA program for the University of Phoenix for over 30 years.

I guess I was destined to return to the creative side of life, now at the ripe old age of 81. Old dogs, new tricks? Perhaps in this case. Yes, this is not your typical "about the author." Blame the weather.

VOICES PUBLICATION COLLECTION

Beach Voices

Doors We Go Through

The Chair Has Something To Say

Walk In My Garden

What's In The Box?

Clothes Get Testy

Food Talks Back

Fences, In And Out

What Hands Hold

ALSO BY BRAD AYERS

A Life's Journey

Beach Voices

The Chair Has Something to Say

Walk in My Garden

What's in the Box?

Food Talks Back

Doors We Go Through

Fences In and Out

Clothes Get Testy

Made in the USA
Columbia, SC
19 July 2024

38830999R00036